KT-493-162

THE BRIGHTER BOROUGH

First published in 2003 by
Franklin Watts
96 Leonard Street
London
EC2A 4XD

Franklin Watts Australia
45–51 Huntley Street
Alexandria
NSW 2015

A CIP catalogue record for this book is available from the British Library.

ISBN 0 7496 4889 9 (hbk)
ISBN 0 7496 5130 X (pbk)

Series Editor: Jackie Hamley
Series Advisor: Dr Barrie Wade
Cover Design: Jason Anscomb
Design: Peter Scoulding

Printed in Hong Kong / China

In memory of my father, Peter Turner,
who was so special. – HR
"He spoke for those that could not speak
and guided those that could not see."

Flynn Flies High

by Hilary Robinson and Tim Archbold

W
FRANKLIN WATTS
LONDON • SYDNEY

No one at school wanted to be Flynn's friend...

...except Jack.

Flynn didn't come to school every day. He didn't wear the right clothes, or do very well in class.

Some children talked behind his back, and wouldn't sit next to him in lessons.

Flynn was good at some things.

He could do back flips...

...and cartwheels.

But because he couldn't play football, no one wanted him in their team...

...except Jack.

Then Flynn was away from school one day, and the day after that, and the day after that.

In fact, he was away for weeks. And Jack was the only person who noticed.

Then, during football training, everyone watched as a travelling circus went past.

They were all quiet until someone shouted: "Look! There's Flynn! And look...

...his house has wheels!"

And everyone laughed...

...except Jack.

The other children soon forgot about Flynn. Until, one day, heavy rain made the football pitch so wet that no one could train.

They were all moaning when someone joked that Flynn's house would be stuck in a field. And everyone laughed... except Jack.

Then someone suggested going
to the circus instead.
So off they went!

Everyone got excited when the ringmaster cried: “Welcome everyone! Welcome to our show!

To help get us off to a swinging start, please give a big welcome to Flynn the Flying Trapeze!"

For once,

no one said a word.

After a dazzling display of
daring dives, twists and turns,

swings through hoops high,

high above the crowd,

Flynn landed and bowed.

The crowd cheered and yelled for more. The ringmaster said, "Flynn! Flynn! Listen to that roar!

You must have lots of your friends out there. Why don't you invite them to join you in the ring?"

Flynn simply smiled and said, "Yes, I've got lots of good friends, but I didn't have any at school before...

…except Jack!”

Hopscotch has been specially designed to fit the requirements of the National Literacy Strategy. It offers real books by top authors and illustrators for children developing their reading skills.

There are .14 other Hopscotch stories to choose from:

Marvin, the Blue Pig — 0 7496 4619 5 (pbk)
Written by Karen Wallace, illustrated by Lisa Williams

Plip and Plop — 0 7496 4620 9 (pbk)
Written by Penny Dolan, illustrated by Lisa Smith

The Queen's Dragon — 0 7496 4618 7 (pbk)
Written by Anne Cassidy, illustrated by Gwyneth Williamson

Flora McQuack — 0 7496 4621 7 (pbk)
Written by Penny Dolan, illustrated by Kay Widdowson

Willie the Whale — 0 7496 4623 3 (pbk)
Written by Joy Oades, illustrated by Barbara Vagnozzi

Naughty Nancy — 0 7496 4622 5 (pbk)
Written by Anne Cassidy, illustrated by Desideria Guicciardini

Run! — 0 7496 4705 1 (pbk)
Written by Sue Ferraby, illustrated by Fabiano Fiorin

The Playground Snake — 0 7496 4706 X (pbk)
Written by Brian Moses, illustrated by David Mostyn

"Sausages!" — 0 7496 4707 8 (pbk)
Written by Anne Adeney, illustrated by Roger Fereday

The Truth about Hansel and Gretel — 0 7496 4708 6 (pbk)
Written by Karina Law, illustrated by Elke Counsell

Pippin's Big Jump — 0 7496 4710 8 (pbk)
Written by Hilary Robinson, illustrated by Sarah Warburton

Whose Birthday Is It? — 0 7496 4709 4 (pbk)
Written by Sherryl Clark, illustrated by Jan Smith

The Princess and the Frog — 0 7496 4891 0 (hbk)
Written by Margaret Nash, illustrated by Martin Remphry — 0 7496 5129 6 (pbk)

Clever Cat — 0 7496 4890 2 (hbk)
Written by Karen Wallace, illustrated by Anni Axworthy — 0 7496 5131 8 (pbk)